TEENY WEENIES

THE EIGHTH OCTOPUS

AND OTHER STORIES

STARSCAPE BOOKS BY DAVID LUBAR

Novels

Emperor of the Universe
Flip
Hidden Talents
True Talents

Monsterrific Tales

Hyde and Shriek
The Vanishing Vampire
The Unwilling Witch
The Wavering Werewolf
The Gloomy Ghost
The Bully Bug

Nathan Abercrombie, Accidental Zombie series

My Rotten Life
Dead Guy Spy
Goop Soup
The Big Stink
Enter the Zombie

Story Collections

Attack of the Vampire Weenies and Other Warped and Creepy Tales

The Battle of the Red Hot Pepper Weenies and Other Warped and Creepy Tales

Beware the Ninja Weenies and Other Warped and Creepy Tales

Check out the Library Weenies and Other Warped and Creepy Tales

The Curse of the Campfire Weenies and Other Warped and Creepy Tales

In the Land of the Lawn Weenies and Other Warped and Creepy Tales

Invasion of the Road Weenies and Other Warped and Creepy Tales

Strikeout of the Bleacher Weenies and Other Warped and Creepy Tales

Wipeout of the Wireless Weenies and Other Warped and Creepy Tales

Teeny Weenies: The Boy Who Cried Wool and Other Stories

Teeny Weenies: Fishing for Pets and Other Stories

Teeny Weenies: Freestyle Frenzy and Other Stories

Teeny Weenies: The Intergalactic Petting Zoo and Other Stories

Teeny Weenies: My Favorite President and Other Stories

TEENY WEENIES

THE EIGHTH OCTOPUS

AND OTHER STORIES

DAVID LUBAR

ILLUSTRATED BY BILL MAYER

STARSCAPE

A TOM DOHERTY ASSOCIATES BOOK

NEW YORK

THE EIGHTH OCTOPUS AND OTHER STORIES

Copyright © 2020 by David Lubar

Illustrations copyright © 2020 Bill Mayer

A Starscape Book
Published by Tom Doherty Associates
120 Broadway
New York, NY 10271

www.tor-forge.com

The Library of Congress Cataloging-in-Publication Data
is available upon request.

ISBN 978-1-250-18786-4 (hardcover)
ISBN 978-1-250-18787-1 (ebook)

Our books may be purchased in bulk for promotional, educational, or business use. Please contact your local bookseller or the Macmillan Corporate and Premium Sales Department at 1-800-221-7945, extension 5442, or by email at MacmillanSpecialMarkets@macmillan.com.

First Edition: May 2020

Printed in the United States of America

0 9 8 7 6 5 4 3 2 1

For Joelle and Alison, full circle

CONTENTS

TEENY WEENIES

THE EIGHTH OCTOPUS

AND OTHER STORIES

THE EIGHTH
OCTOPUS

"I hope it's not another octopus," Adam said as he opened the birthday present from his great-aunt Sophie. He spoke quietly so she wouldn't hear.

Every year, Great-aunt Sophie brought Adam an octopus. She was an oceanographer, and had set up a special saltwater tank when she'd brought the first octopus. Adam had been too young to remember that first birthday, but his parents had taken plenty of photos.

This was his eighth birthday, so he already had seven of these unusual presents, which seemed like at least six more than anyone would need. Seven octopi occupied the tank in Adam's bedroom. Fourteen eyes blinked at him each morning. Fifty-six tentacles rippled in the water, waving at  him each day as he went out to play.

Seven octopi.

Now, it was October eighth, and Adam unwrapped his unsurprising eighth octopi.

"Oh, this one's very pretty," Adam's mother said with barely a shudder in her voice as she  leaned over his shoulder and stared down at the half-open package. "What do we say?" she asked, nudging Adam in the back.

"Thank you very much, Great-aunt Sophie," Adam said as the octopus helped unwrap itself.

"My pleasure," Great-aunt Sophie said. "A child can never have too many octopi."

"Guess I'll put it in the tank with the others." Adam carried the plastic bowl up the steps and into his room.

"Join your friends," Adam said as he tipped the octopus into the tank.

Now eight octopi occupied the tank in Adam's room.

Sixteen eyes blinked at him.

Sixty-four tentacles rippled in the water.

Each tentacle touched every other tentacle one at a time, creating more tentacle touches than Adam could count. The water bubbled and frothed. The octopi moved closer together.

And closer.

Adam gasped. The air flared and glared with a giant octopossible flash. Adam staggered back and blinked. He blinked again, but what he saw wouldn't blink away. When he looked into the tank after the last of the frothy bubbles had burst, he found a single amaz-

ing octopus with sixty-four octotangled tentacles, sixteen octoblinkable eyes, and eight octo-openable octoclosable mouths, all on one octo-impossible slightly octagonal head.

Unlike the seven uncoupled octopi that had each seemed content to lie at the bottom of the tank, Adam's newest octopus—an octo-product of all the previous octopi—appeared to want to wander.

It hoisted its octoriffic body from the depths of the tank and flipped over the edge, bouncing to the floor with a gentle octosplat not unlike the landing a wet bath sponge might make on a bathroom floor.

"I think I'll call you Armando," Adam said, liking the way Armando started with an *A* just like Adam, and even better yet, the way Armando started with an *Arm*.

Armando waved a half-dozen tentacles in agreement, then octowaddled toward the door, slipping and sliding, rippling and rolling, twitching and tumbling as he mastered the art of traveling on land.

"Wait for me," Adam called. He pumped his two legs to catch up with Armando, who was already octorolling down the steps like a Slinky made of spaghetti. As Adam reached the bottom of the stairs, Armando extended a tentacle and took Adam's hand. Together, they strolled outside.

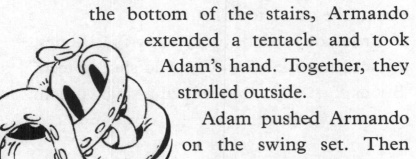

Adam pushed Armando on the swing set. Then Armando pushed Adam, and several of his friends, all at once. They took turns on the slide, going faster each time thanks to the slight smears of octoslime, which made the metal slick and slippery. After that, Adam grabbed his base-ball glove from the house and they played catch, followed by badminton, hopscotch, and jacks.

They played until it was

time for dinner. And when dinner was done, Armando octocut the cake.

With Armando's help, Adam got ready for bed in record time.

"What an octoperfect birthday," Adam said as he crawled under the covers. "Good night," he called to Armando.

Armando waved back, sixty-four times. Adam shut two eyes. Armando shut sixteen. But as they slept, they shared a single dream of octodays ahead.

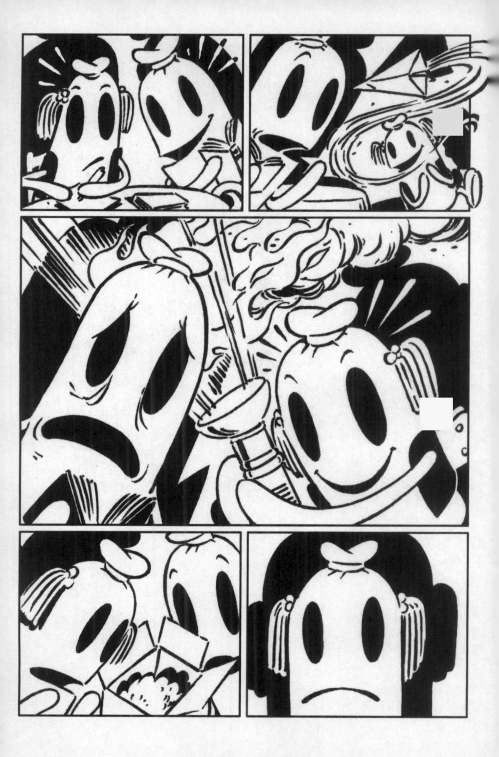

THE POWER OF WORDS

I wonder whether each of us has a special word that triggers magical things. I have one. But there are two problems with my word. First, it doesn't work if I say it myself. I guess that would be too easy. If you could say your own spell, everyone would be doing magic all the time. Second, it's not a great word. I wish my word had been FLY! or GOLD! I'm not that lucky. And my word only seems to work when it is shouted by my icky stepbrother, Baldridge. I've been listening carefully ever since I discovered my word, and nothing happens if anyone else says it.

Here's how I found out about the word. We were sitting at the kitchen table. Baldridge was helping me with my math homework, because he's some sort of math genius, and I'm some sort of math not-genius. He wasn't doing it because he loved me with all of his heart. He was doing it because Dad made him.

Still, that was no reason for him to shout at me every time I stopped to think. I was trying my best to understand how to solve a word problem about two trains that had no business traveling at totally different speeds or leaving their stations at such inconvenient times. I'd managed to turn the words into an equation. But I wasn't sure what to do next. It was hard to remember all the math rules when Baldridge kept jabbering, and pointing at my paper.

"Think, Lisa," he said. "I already told you that you have to balance the fractions on both sides. That's why it's called an *equation*. It has to stay equal. Get it?"

"Uh, yeah." I took a sip of my orange juice. It was fresh squeezed, with lots of pulp. Dad might be really strict about schoolwork, but Mom is great about snacks. She never bought the thick stuff you had to mix with water.

I put the glass down, picked up my pencil, and tried to follow Baldridge's directions. I knew I had to subtract the same amount from each side. But it was all so confusing. How do you subtract one-seventh from $3x$? I put down my pencil and picked up my glass.

"Concentrate!" Baldridge shouted.

I took another sip of juice, and nearly choked.

Something had happened to it. It was too thick, and too sweet. Like syrup. Or like . . .

. . . *concentrate* . . .

No way.

I took a smaller sip, and let it sit in my mouth.

Way.

"Right back." I hopped out of my chair and went to the sink.

"You'll never learn anything if you keep running around," Baldridge said.

"I'm not running around," I said. I added water to my glass and took a sip. That was better. It wasn't as fresh and amazing tasting as before, but at least it wasn't so sweet and thick that it would make me gag.

I got through three problems and four-fifths of the juice in my glass—see, I can do fractions—when Baldridge shouted, "Concentrate!" again.

And the juice responded.

I looked at Baldrdidge's coffee cup. I could tell his drink hadn't gotten concentrated. It only happened to mine.

For the next tutoring session, I made hot cocoa, even though the weather was warm and sunny. It was delicious to start with, but it was amazing when it got concentrated. I went through three more weeks of that before I got tired of the cocoa. That's when I realized I needed to do some research. There had to be something even better to cast the spell on. I started searching for information about concentrated things. After skimming  through tons of information about fruit juices, I stumbled across a sentence that made me shout out loud: Diamonds are the most concentrated form of pure carbon.

My shout was followed by a thought: *I'm going to be so rich, I'll hire people to do my math for me.*

I needed carbon. That was easy. My folks had a grill in the backyard. There was a bag of charcoal for it in the garage. I got some of the briquettes and crushed them with a rock, then put the charcoal dust into a small box.

Right before my next tutoring session, I put the box on the table.

"I'm tired of pushing you," Baldridge said when he took a seat at the table. He pulled a book out of his backpack. It wasn't a math book. It was a novel. "If you fool around, I'm just going to sit here and read. You're the one who'll get the bad grade."

Oh, great. I started working on the first problem, but then stared out the window. After a while, I snuck a look at Baldridge. His nose was buried deep in his book. I got back to work.

Then, I started humming. He ignored me.

I folded one of my worksheets into a paper airplane and threw it at him.

He didn't even look up. But I could tell he was struggling to make it seem like he wasn't noticing me. If I pushed him a bit harder, he'd break. And I'd be rich.

I looked around for something to play with. There was a flashlight on top of the refrigerator. I grabbed it, sat down, and shined the light up at my chin. "Look, I'm spooky!" I said.

No reaction.

"Woooooo . . . I'm a monster!"

Nothing.

I thrust the flashlight out and shined it up under Baldridge's chin, blocking his book.

"Now you're a monster!"

"Stop it!" he screamed, throwing the book down. "Concentrate!"

 I staggered back. He'd startled me. But that was okay. He'd also finally done what I wanted. I was about to become the richest girl in town.

The thrill of success didn't last long. It vanished in a flash. Or a flashlight. The beam turned red.

Later, I learned that a LASER is concentrated light.

That was later. Right now, what I learned was that a LASER can set hair on fire. It was a good thing I'd jumped when Baldridge startled me. Otherwise, I might have set his chin on fire. It was bad enough I'd scorched his hair.

Baldridge refused to tutor me after that. He doesn't even speak to me, most of the time. There's no way I'll ever get him to shout the magic word again. And as for the diamond, I'd overlooked one tiny word. I needed *pure* carbon for that to work. It turns out briquettes aren't pure.

There was nothing sparkly in the box.

No diamond. No magic. No tutor.

I guess it was up to me to concentrate on my work for myself from now on.

THE MIDDLEMAN

It was the hottest morning yet. Phil noticed that as soon as he woke up. *This will be great,* he thought as he got dressed. The temperature was sure to break ninety degrees before noon. It was perfect weather for a small-business owner.

"Where are you headed, Phil?" his mom asked as he raced through the kitchen.

"I'm going to sell lemonade to the tourists," he said, opening the refrigerator.

"You'll need lemons."

"Oops. We're out of them?"

His mother nodded. "You'll have to buy some more at the store."

"No problem." Phil ran back up-stairs, got money from his bank, then stepped outside. The heat hit him in the face like a wall of lava. Fantastic—a couple of weeks like this and he'd finally have enough for a bike.

People were already walking from town. Phil lived between town and the beach. There was a constant flow of foot traffic. It was a perfect place to sell lemonade. He bought a large bag of lemons at the market, then headed home. As he passed his favorite corner, he saw the worst thing in the world: someone was already there. It was Johnny Nelson, selling lemonade at Phil's favorite spot.

"Hey Johnny, that's my spot."

"I don't see your name on it," Johnny said. "Besides, you know what they say. 'If you snooze, you lose.'" Johnny smiled to show he wasn't trying to be mean.

"Very funny." Phil was beginning to wonder if he had gotten too late a start. He headed toward the next corner to see if it was vacant.  Half a block away, he knew it was taken. There was Cheryl Stein, another kid from the neighborhood, selling lemonade.

"Are you planning to stay all day?" he asked her.

She nodded, then said, "But if I decide to quit early, you can have my spot."

Phil thanked her, then ran to the other end of the block, only to see Javier Lopez doing business. On the next block, the Gandy twins were selling lemonade by the gallon to crowds of thirsty tourists.

Great, he thought. It was the hottest day of the year and he didn't have a spot. To top it off, he was lugging around a big bag of lemons. This was not going to be his day. He turned around and headed back toward his home.

"How's business, Javier?" he asked as he walked by. Just because he was out of luck was no reason not to wish his friends would do well.

"Best day ever," Javier said. "It's so good, I'm running low on stuff. You won't steal my spot if I run to the store, will you?"

"I wouldn't do that," Phil told him. He might be tempted, but it wouldn't be right to take someone's spot, even if lemonade was selling like hotcakes. But maybe he could keep the day from being a total loss. "Javier, instead of running to the store, let me sell you some lemons."

"How much?"

Phil paused to think. The bag had cost three dollars and it contained twelve lemons. That meant each lemon cost him twenty-five cents. "How about thirty cents each?" Phil asked.

"OK, that's fair. I think it's a bit more than the store charges, but I won't lose all the sales I'd miss by going there myself. You've got a deal."

As Phil put the money in his pocket, he realized how wonderful his idea really was. Each kid selling lemonade would run out of lemons. They'd also run out of sugar and ice. They might even need cups if they didn't plan ahead. This was a lot nicer than competing for a spot. To top it off, the better his friends did, the better he would do. He couldn't sell lemonade today, but he could still do business.

Before going home for his wagon and the cooler, he stopped at each stand and found out what was in short supply. The twins needed lemons and ice. Cheryl just needed lemons. Johnny wasn't low on anything yet, but he asked Phil to get him an ice pop.

"Back so soon?" his mom asked when he ran into the house.

"Change of plans," Phil told her. He grabbed a small notebook so he could keep track of his orders.

As he trotted toward the store with his wagon rattling behind him, Phil realized that he liked this new business a lot more than selling lemonade. He wasn't stuck in one place. He could move around. And he knew exactly what he was selling and who was buying. When he got his bike, he'd also buy a basket for it. There was a whole world out there that needed lemons.

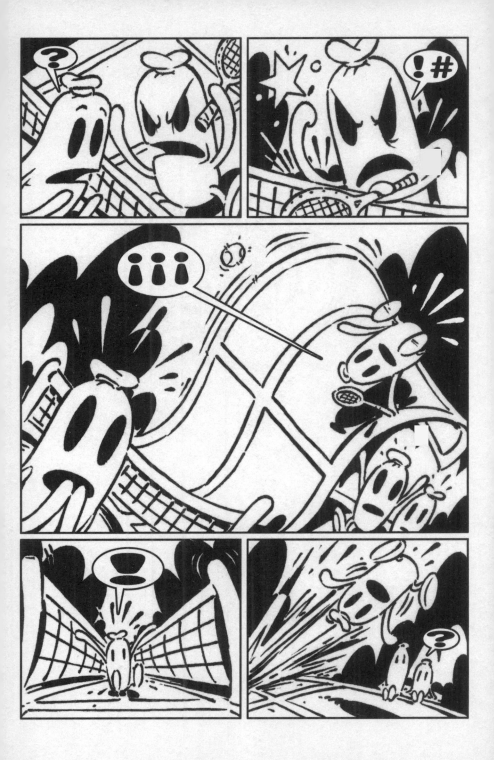

FOR THE LOVE
OF TENNIS

I **love** tennis. I play it every chance I get. But I don't get a lot of chances. Most of my friends are all wrapped up with dance, or cheering, or field hockey. Those are fine. But tennis is where my heart is. Every morning, in the summer, I'll walk over to the school and hit balls against the back wall, by the rear parking lot. It's not as good as playing against someone, but it lets me work on my ground strokes. Then, I'll go to the court by the park. There's only one court, but nobody is ever there in the morning. I'll practice my serve. I'm getting pretty good at that.

And, don't tell anyone, but I talk to the court, like it's my doubles partner. I know that's silly, but I like to think the court is more than a slab of green concrete with white lines and a sagging old net.

Once in a while, someone will show up who wants to play. I like that. I don't care whether it's a beginner or an expert. I can play, and learn stuff, either way. But more often, it's two people who take over the court for singles, or four people who play doubles, leaving me left out.

Today, it was four kids I recognized from school; Ellie Chen, Maria Diaz, Nuveen Patel, and Aaron Wadsworth. They were a year ahead of me, and would be starting seventh grade in the new middle school next fall. I said hi as I walked off the court. They ignored me. I decided to watch them play. That's how much I loved the game.

They were playing boys against girls. Aaron served first. He swatted his opening serve so hard, it smacked into the net. I winced. I could almost feel how

it would sting to be hit by that. He smacked his second serve even harder. It whacked the net, too.

He did the same thing for the next point.

"Hey, it's better to go softer and get the serve in," I said. Everyone knew that. Ellie smiled at me and nodded, but none of them said anything.

The boys lost the first game, naturally. Maria was up next. She also hit her first serve into the net. But she eased up with the second one, and got it in. Aaron smacked it hard. It went right into the net.

"Open up the face of your racket," I said.

I mostly said it to myself, but that would help keep the ball from hitting the net.

Nuveen returned the next serve, hitting it hard to Maria's backhand. She lobbed it right over Aaron, who was at the net. He backed up, jumped, and smashed it— right into the net. He walked over to pick up the ball, and slammed his racket into the net.

"Stupid net!" he yelled. "It's too high!"

It's actually too low, I thought. But I kept my mouth shut.

After Aaron hit his next return right over the fence,  he slammed his racket on the court—not hard enough to break it, but hard enough for me to wince again.

"You're hurting it," I said. I was surprised by my own words. I did sort of think of the court as an old friend. But I knew it really didn't have feelings.

At least, I'd always thought that was true—until now.

As Aaron walked back toward the net, the  center line that divided the service boxes rose up behind him, like a rolling wave swelling across the ocean. My jaw dropped as I watched it roll forward.

"Whoa!" Aaron screamed as the line rammed into him from behind.

The line pushed him hard. He stumbled forward, toward the net. But the net was stretching away from him, pulling against the two end posts as it got dragged back by another part of the center line that had hooked the bottom. It reminded me of a slingshot. The center of the net had stretched all the way back to the end of the service box. The end poles leaned back, tilting the net at an angle, as if waiting for a stone. Or a boy.

The center line rose higher, flipping Aaron into the pocket of the net.

Aaron screamed louder as he landed upside down in a sprawl. He looked like the biggest victim to ever get caught in a spider's web.

There was an amazing *SPROING!* as the line released the net. Aaron shot through the air, tumbling and screaming. He cleared the fence easily, and sailed past the creek before he fell into a pasture. Luckily for him, he landed on a manure pile. That broke his fall.

I looked at the three remaining kids.

"Want to play?" Ellie asked.

"Sure," I said. "I'd love to."

As I walked onto the court, I patted the net, which had returned to its normal position.

"Thanks," I whispered.

As for whether it spoke back, that's my little secret.

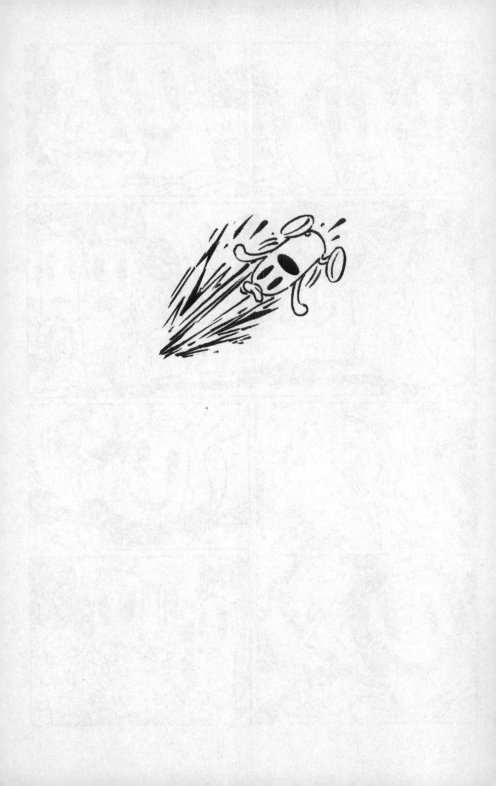

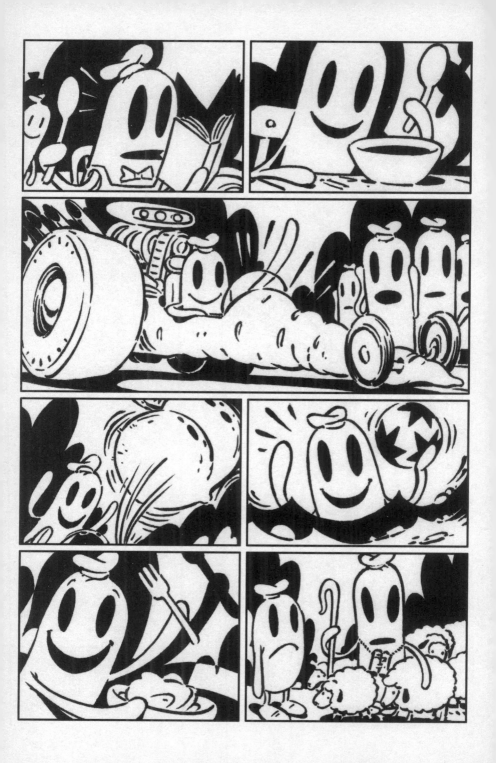

FOODIE DREAMS

It all started with the carrots. Dalton's mom had given his dad a new recipe book, *Dreamy Foods for the Whole Family,* and the next day Dalton's dad made Creamy Dreamy Carrot Soup.

Dalton stared at the orange liquid in his bowl.

"Try it," his dad said.

Dalton shrugged and gave the soup a try. He was relieved that it wasn't bad.

"Tastes pretty good," he said.

That night, he dreamed he walked out of his house and found a giant bright-orange carrot

in his driveway. When he stepped up to the carrot, it made a sound. But not the sort of sound anyone would expect a carrot to make if a carrot could make sounds. It went *VROOOOMMMMM, VROOOMMMMM!*

A door opened in the carrot. Dalton slipped inside and sat on a comfortable seat that smelled like leather. The carrot, which was looking more and more like a fast car, both inside and out, zoomed down the driveway and raced through town, screeching around corners at high speeds.

It was a good dream.

The next afternoon, Dalton's parents told him they were getting a new car. They took him with them to the dealer. The car was

sleek and fast looking. And it was orange, with leather seats.

That's a weird coincidence, Dalton thought.

His dad didn't use the cookbook again for several days. But then, he made Sweet as a Dream Peach Cobbler.

It was sweet and tasty.

Dalton dreamed again.

Once again, the dream started with him walking outside. Instead of a carrot, he saw a peach. The peach started to bounce. It grew larger. It flew toward Dalton. He punched it when it got close to his face. He flinched, expecting to be sprayed with peach juice, but the peach bounced off his fist like a beach ball, flying through the air with an off-center spin. When it hit the ground, it turned red and white and blue. The ground turned into sand. Seagulls screeched and circled. It was a great dream. Dalton loved the beach. He chased the ball into the water and played with it as the waves crashed all around him.

The next morning, when Dalton woke, his parents told him they'd decided to take a trip to the beach.

That night, Dalton looked through the whole cookbook. The car and the beach trip were nice, but he really wanted a dog. He turned page after page, looking at the recipes. Finally, he found exactly what he needed: Shepherd's Pie to Feast Your Eye. Dalton had never heard of that dish before, but when he read the list of ingredients, he saw it was made with ground beef and mashed potatoes. It sounded tasty. Best of all, Dalton's favorite dog was a German shepherd.

"This has to work," he whispered. He left the book open to that recipe. And he mentioned hamburgers and french fries every time he talked with his dad.

After three days, his dad finally said, "I think I can make something even better than burgers and fries."

"Really?" Dalton asked, acting his best to seem surprised.

"I saw an interesting recipe for ground beef and mashed potatoes, all in a pie crust. Sound good?"

"Sure," Dalton said.

And it was good.

His dream that night started with him walking out his front door. His heart leaped when he saw a dog waiting there. It wasn't a German shepherd, but that was fine. It was a beautiful dog with a black and white coat.

"Hi," Dalton said.

He held his hand out for the dog to sniff. The dog ran off. Dalton chased it around the house, through the backyard, and into the field behind the house.

The dog ran up to a man. Dalton skidded to a stop as he tried to make sense of what he was seeing. The man was standing in front of a flock of sheep. He was holding a long stick in one hand, and binoculars in the other.

Dalton noticed the binoculars were pointed at him. "Who are you?" he asked.

The man spoke four words that crushed Dalton's dream—from the inside.  "I'm a shepherd spy."

"Shepherd spy . . ." Dalton said. "Shepherd's pie . . ."

"Right," the man said.

"Can I pet your dog?" Dalton asked.

"No. Sorry. He's working," the man said as the dog chased after a stray sheep.

"Who are you spying on?" Dalton asked, though he was afraid he knew the answer already.

"On you," the man said.

Dalton didn't like the idea of being watched. "Who are you doing it for?"

"Anyone who might be interested," the man said. "Your parents. Your teachers. Santa. Your friends, if you do something they might not like."

"For how long?" Dalton asked.

"Forever," the man said.

Dalton awoke to the sound of his own scream. He rolled out of bed, ran to the window, and looked at the field behind his house.

No dog.

No sheep.

Dalton sighed, feeling relieved. And then a flash caught his eye, at the farthest edge of the field, like sunlight glinting off binoculars.

"Great," Dalton muttered. He pulled his curtains closed. But from that day on, he could never escape the feeling that someone was keeping an eye on him.

BAIT 4 SALE

Danny sat in the shade and watched the fisherman walk down the path to the edge of the lake. When the man got close enough, Danny patted the small cooler on the ground next to him and said, "Need to buy any bait, mister?"

"No, thanks," the man said. He held up a Styrofoam container the size of a coffee cup. "I brought enough."

"Well, I'll be here if you need more," Danny said. He sat by a tree and watched as the man put down his tackle box and removed a wriggling night crawler from the container.

The man flipped the bail on his spinning reel and cast his bait out, then turned toward Danny and asked, "How are they biting around here?"

"Pretty good," Danny said. He yawned and stretched, raising both hands high above his head, then settled back against the tree. "There are some really big fish in the lake. Honest. Last week, I saw a guy land one that must have been at least—"

Danny was interrupted by a splash. He glanced at the lake. So did the fisherman. "Wow!" the man said, pointing toward the water. "Did you see that?"

"Yup." Danny gazed at a spot about fifty feet from the shore. Ripples broke the calm surface. It looked like something huge had leaped out of the water. "Might be a large-mouth," Danny told the man. "The bass get pretty big out here."

The man quickly reeled in his line. He brought it in so fast that the worm got pulled off. Danny watched, noticing how excited the man was as he grabbed another worm from his container and put it on the hook. The man cast too hard as he aimed for the center of the dying ripples. His hook reached the water near the spot, but his worm flew off in a different direction, dropping into the lake with a *plop*.

The man muttered something and reeled in again. Danny watched. Twice more, the man cast too hard and lost his worm. Finally, he managed to reach the spot.

"Lot of little bait stealers out there," Danny said. He knew the lake was filled with bluegills and other sunfish that could snatch a large worm right off a hook.

The man quickly lost four more worms as the sunfish stripped his bait. "Maybe I'll try another spot," he grumbled as he glared at his empty hook.

"Yeah, I'll bet that big fish is gone," Danny said. He yawned and stretched again.

The man looked over toward him. Before he could speak, there was another splash, bigger than the first. The man stared at the water for a second, then dug his fingers into his bait container. His actions grew more frantic as he pawed through the soil in the cup. Finally, he turned the cup over, dumping the contents on the ground. He knelt and sifted through the dark mound. "Hey, I'm all out. I'll buy some of your worms," he said to Danny. "How much?"

"Five bucks," Danny said.

The man shook his head. "That's kind of expensive."

 "That's up to you." While Danny waited for the man to make up his mind, he enjoyed a leisurely yawn and stretch.

There was another huge splash

 from the lake. Without saying anything more, the man took out his wallet and gave Danny the money. "Thanks," Danny said, handing the man a package of bait from the cooler.

The man fished for another hour, and went through three containers of worms. He never caught the big fish. Finally, he gave up. Danny watched him walk off.

A moment later, Danny's friend Tommy walked up to him, cutting through the bushes on the side of the lake. "How's business?" Tommy asked.

"Great," Danny said, holding up a fistful of money. "That guy bought three containers." He looked down the path. "Hey, here comes another customer."

"Okay, but let's switch," Tommy said, rubbing his right shoulder with his left hand. "My arm's getting tired."

"Sure," Danny said. "You sell the bait for

a while. I'll go behind the bushes, wait for your signal, and throw the rocks in the water." Danny whistled happily as he hurried to the hiding place. He really enjoyed the bait business.

THE LIFE OF PIE

My mom makes the best cherry pie.

Whenever I get a slice, she laughs and says, "Sophia, you'd eat a whole pie if I let you."

I always want to laugh back and say, "I'd eat two pies!" But it's not nice to talk when your mouth is full, and that's how I like my mouth to be when I'm dealing with pie.

I'm especially happy when Mom puts sour cherries in her pie. They used to be harder to find than the sweet ones, but they make an amazing pie. I say *used to* because we moved to a new house last winter. And I guess *new* isn't the right word, since the house is really old. It was a farmhouse, long ago. They grew corn and soybeans in the fields. We know that because the farmers kept a record of their crops. But they also planted fruit trees near the house. There are apples, pears, and some peaches. All of those are great, but the tree that excited me the most was the sour-cherry tree. There's just one, but it has a ton of fruit on it.

I guess now it has half a ton left, because the cherries finally got ripe enough to pick. I gathered two whole buckets of them this morning. And then, my sister, Inez, and I pitted them. She loves pie as much as I do. Mom baked a pie this afternoon, using six cups of the cherries. She froze the rest, so we can have more pies all year round.

I couldn't wait until dinner. Mom likes to bake, but Dad likes to cook. He also likes to say, "Cooking is an art. Baking is a science."

Tonight, he made lasagna. I love his lasagna, and I usually enjoy every bite. But this time I rushed through it because I was really just waiting for dessert.

Finally, Mom brought out the pie. She gave me a big slice. Inez got one, too. But Mom cut only two slices.

"Where's yours?" I asked. I know this is terrible, but I was secretly hoping Mom and Dad had decided they didn't feel like cherry pie, which meant Inez and I would get it all. Not that we'd eat it all in one day, but leftover pie is just as wonderful as fresh pie.

"We have to run to the store before it closes," Mom said. "We're almost out of milk."

So the folks headed out, and I headed for my slice of pie.

As I lifted my fork, the pie said, "Don't hurt me!"

I jerked back in my seat and dropped my fork. My amazement

was quickly replaced by suspicion. I looked at Inez. Maybe she'd been secretly learning ventriloquism.

But Inez was staring back at me, looking so startled I knew she wasn't acting. If she opened her mouth any wider, her nose would fall into it.

"Did you hear that?" I asked.

She nodded. "Did you?"

"Yeah." I picked up my fork and moved it toward the flaky crust.

"Stop!" the pie screamed. "Or I'll bite you back!"

 "Let's get out of here!" I leaped off my seat, grabbed Inez's hand, and ran to the porch.

"What should we do?" she asked.

"Let's just wait until Mom and Dad get back," I said.

"Good idea." She hopped up on the old bench that was next to the door.

I joined her.

"Get off me! I can't breathe!"

I leaped up. So did Inez. We stared at the bench. The color of the wood and the pattern of the grain were familiar. Our old house had cabinets made of cherry wood.

"I think it's cherry," I said.

 "I think we should wait in the driveway," Inez said.

That seemed like a good idea. There was a hoop on the garage. We shot baskets while we waited, even though neither of us felt like playing.

When the folks got back, Mom asked, "How was the pie?"

"Amazing . . ." I said. I wasn't sure what to tell them. I didn't think they'd believe us if we told them the pie had talked to us. But, in a moment, they'd hear it themselves.

When we reached the kitchen, Dad said, "I wish you girls would remember to rinse your plates after you eat."

"But . . ." I stared at the table. Our plates were still there. But they were empty.

"Tasty," someone whispered.

I followed the sound. And then, I had to force myself not to scream. There was a ghost in the corner. I knew it was a ghost, because I could see all the way through him.

Inez let out a small gasp and grabbed my arm, so I knew she saw it, too.

I almost screamed a second time when I spotted the blood covering the ghost's chin. Then, I realized it wasn't blood. It was juice from the cherries. The ghost had gobbled down both pieces of pie after scaring us out of the kitchen.

"You tricked us!" I shouted.

The ghost shrugged.

Mom and Dad stared at me. I guess they couldn't see the ghost.

"Just kidding," I said.

And then, I had to watch my parents enjoy their slices of pie.

"This is great," Dad said. "But I can't wait for the peaches to be ready. I think that's my favorite."

I think it's mine now, too. I just hope the ghost doesn't feel the same way.

THE LANGUAGE OF MUSIC

Anna missed her piano. For two weeks, her parents had been dragging her all around Europe, constantly telling her that this vacation was a wonderful experience and the trip of a lifetime. Worse, her brother, Orville, seemed to think he was some sort of language expert. Wherever they went, Orville kept getting them lost by misunderstanding directions and signs. He'd gotten them lost in Spain, France, and Portugal, so far. Now, he was in the process of getting them lost in Italy. To top it off, every chance he had, he made fun of her for not knowing any foreign languages.

Some vacation this was turning out to be.

"I'm sure it's just down here," Orville said, pointing to the corner ahead of them. "That's what the man said."

Anna hoped he was right. They'd been walking forever, trying to find this restaurant. Her parents had really wanted to go there. A friend back home had told them, "If you are ever in Florence, be sure to eat at La Fontana."

So here they were, trying to follow directions that Orville claimed he understood perfectly.

"Maybe you should ask someone else," Anna said as they found themselves at the end of another street that didn't go anywhere.

"Why don't *you* ask?" Orville sneered at her. "Let's see how well you do?"

"Now, kids . . ." Anna's dad said. "Let's not fight."

"I'll ask," Anna said. She'd had it with Orville and his attitude. But who could she ask? She looked around.

There was an old man walking toward her. She went up to him, smiled, and asked, "La Fontana?" At the same time, she made eating motions, pretending to hold a knife and fork.

The man grinned, nodded, and then replied in a stream of rapid Italian. Anna shrugged. The man repeated what he'd said. Anna shrugged again. She wished he'd speak more slowly. If she could hear each word separately, she thought she might at least be able to guess some of what he was saying. More than that, she wished she was back home playing her piano.

"Slower, please," she said.

It was the man's turn to respond with a shrug. He didn't understand her.

Anna thought about her piano again. That thought gave her an idea. She could see the word in her mind, just the way it was written on some of her music. She looked at the man and said, *"Adagio."*

"Adagio," he said, grinning

at her. And then he repeated the instructions, but much more slowly.

It worked, Anna thought. She'd seen the word many times. It was used when music was supposed to be played slowly. As she listened to the man, she realized that there were other Italian words she knew from her music, like *prima, facile,* and *tutti*. Between the instructions on her sheet music, the names of many songs, and the words for parts of instruments, Anna discovered she had a great vocabulary. Italian wasn't such a hard language, after all.

When the man finished giving her the directions, Anna turned back to her family and said, "We make the next left, then go over the bridge. The restaurant is four blocks away, on the right."

Anna turned back to the man. She remembered another word. She hadn't learned it in her musical studies, but it was the right word for the moment. *"Grazie,"* she said, thanking the man.

"Prego," the man replied.

"This way," Anna said. She led her family to the restaurant. Behind her, Orville was pleasantly silent for once. Apparently, he couldn't think of a single word to say in any language.

APRIL FOOLS

Some kids love Halloween more than any other holiday. Some love Thanksgiving the most, or the Fourth of July. Not me. Those are all great holidays. I like candy and turkey and fireworks. But, more than anything else, I love playing pranks on people. I was born for April Fools' Day. And it was almost here. Today was the last day in March. Tomorrow was the day I'd been waiting for all year.

I like to play pranks on my parents and my friends, of course, but it's especially fun to play jokes on my little brother, Ethan. He's only six, so he's pretty easy to fool. It was also fun to scare him a bit ahead of time.

Right after Mom and Dad tucked him in and came downstairs, I said, "I should tell Ethan a bedtime story."

"How sweet of you," Mom said as I headed upstairs.

Oh, it would be sweet, all right. And not just tonight. I would have a totally sweet time tomorrow. But Ethan wouldn't. He'd be suffering through a whole day of jokes.

When I got to his room he was half asleep, looking all cute, innocent, and helpless in his spaceman pajamas, covered with spinning planets and zooming comets. Ethan is crazy about space. I think that's because he's as weird as an alien from Mars.

"It's almost here," I said, making my voice mysterious and spooky.

"I know," he said.

That surprised me. Ethan usually seemed totally clueless about holidays. But I kept going. "April Fools' Day is coming, especially for you."

Before I could tack on an evil laugh, he said, "I've been waiting all my life for this."

That made no sense. He was six. So he'd already lived through April Fools' Days a bunch of times. Though I guess he wouldn't remember the first two or three. "All your life?" I asked.

"Ever since last week when I was born," he said.

That was so weird, I decided to ignore it. Then, I figured out what was going on. He was trying to pull an April Fools' joke on me. Good luck with that. First of all, it wasn't April Fools' Day until tomorrow. And second, I was the expert. Nobody was going to fool me. Especially not a little kid who still needed help tying his shoes and didn't seem to know how long ago he'd been born. I was just way too clever to be tricked by him. But I decided to play along, because it would be fun watching his pathetic effort to fool me. And maybe it would give me an idea for an awesome joke to play on him tomorrow.

"You were born last week?" I asked.

He nodded. "That's in Zooper-snooper weeks," he said. "Our days are longer than yours, Earthling. But we have many of the same holidays."

"That's great . . ." I struggled to keep from laughing. Zoopersnooper— what a ridiculous little-kid idea for the name of an alien planet. I would have done way better. Zardox. Phongo. Mixultra. See? I wasn't just great at coming up with pranks. I was also totally awesome at making up names for planets.

"See you tomorrow," I said as I headed out of his room.

Now, I just needed to think up the perfect stunt to play on my *alien* brother.

Got it! I'm always awake before him, even though he goes to bed earlier. Tomorrow morning, I'd sneak into his room right before he woke up, and scare him with an alien mask. I didn't have one, but I could make something pretty easily. It didn't even have to be all that good, since it would be sort of dark in his room in the morning.

We had a craft box downstairs, with all sorts of supplies. It wasn't hard to cut a mask out of some green felt, and give it huge white eyes with slitted black pupils. I poked a small hole on each side of the mask and tied some rubber bands together to make a strap.

The next morning, I slipped the mask over my face and crept into Ethan's room. Then I stood over his bed and got ready to give him the scare of a lifetime. I had to keep from laughing and spoiling the surprise. This was going to be amazing.

"April Fools!"

I froze.

Ethan had sat up fast and shouted the words before I could say them. He thrust out both hands, pointing all ten fingers at me. I was dazzled by a flash as tiny lightning bolts shot from his hands.

And then, I was falling.

I was so startled, I screamed. I tried to figure out where I was. That wasn't easy, because I was spinning as I fell. I screamed again when the terrifying answer hit me. I was plunging down from the clouds, right toward the mouth of an active volcano that was spewing red-hot lava into the air.

"Help!" I screamed.

Lava shot up at me.

Ethan stood on the rim of the volcano, laughing. The heat didn't seem to bother him. He had a stick in one hand and a bag of marshmallows in the other. I realized he was toasting one of them over the volcano.

Just when the heat became almost unbearable, Ethan shouted, "April Fools!" and thrust his hands out again, zapping me with more lightning bolts.

After another dazzling flash, I was bobbing in the ocean. But I wasn't on Earth. The water was red. But not red enough to hide the worst part. Huge eels with hundreds of teeth raced toward me, snapping their jaws.

Ethan floated next to me, eating marshmallows. "Isn't this great?" he asked. "I really fooled you."

"No! It's not great. Bring me home," I begged.

"No way," he said. "I love April Fools' Day."

Dark shapes wriggled toward me beneath the surface of the water. Right before the first eel chomped me, Ethan sent us into freezing cold outer space, and then into a jungle filled with giant mosquitoes. He let one of them stab me in the leg before zipping us to a  nightmare of a planet that was far too close to its sun. He held up a bag of popcorn and laughed as the kernels popped from the heat.

I closed my eyes and gritted my teeth. *Hang on,* I told myself. *It's just one day. And then it will be over.*

But hours later, after I'd suffered countless

horrors, I realized something. Ethan was six. At least, he was six in Earth years. But he'd said he'd been born last week. I tried to do the math as I hurtled toward a black hole that threatened to rip my atoms apart, and then got dragged by wild creatures across an endless valley of sharp gravel, but it was hard to think when Ethan kept shouting, "April Fools!" and laughing hysteri-

cally as he munched a variety of snacks.

Six years was . . . I did a rough estimate. Six times three-hundred-sixty . . . It was about twenty-one hundred days.

I screamed as I dropped into the gaping jaws of a lizard the size of a small city and slid down its throat.

So, if that was one week for Ethan . . .

I was up to my neck in what seemed to be sewage, struggling to do math while my mind was much more interested in discovering how many different types of screams I could pro-duce.

Twenty-one divided by seven is three.

"No!" I shouted when it hit me that each of his alien days was about three hundred of my Earth days. "Stop!"

Ethan stared at me with eyes that no longer seemed human. Or kind.

"Stop?" He let out a laugh that chilled me, despite the fact that I was currently buried up to my neck in burning sand while centipedes nibbled at my ears. "Are you kidding? We've barely started."

I now knew three things for sure. First, and worst, my little brother really was an alien who was far better than I was at thinking up ways to make his sibling suffer. Second, it was going to be an unimaginably long and totally terrible day. And third, I needed to find a new favorite holiday—assuming I survived this one.

FLAPPING IN THE BREEZE

I have no idea who made the first dare, but somehow or other my friend Jimmy and I ended up right outside of the Parker house. It's haunted. Everyone knows that. That's why nobody goes near it. But there we were, right on the porch.

Jimmy pointed at the door. "Try the knob, Sammy."

"You try it," I said.

I was hoping he'd chicken out. Then we could both go home.

I spun as I heard a flapping sound. "Ghost!" I shouted.

Jimmy dropped into a crouch. "Where?"

I pointed toward the flapping, ready to make a run for safety. But then, I realized there was a ragged old flag on a pole that slanted up from the corner of the house, to the right of the porch. I could feel the breeze on my face. And I could feel my face flush as I watched the flag.

"Never mind," I said.

"Don't do stuff like that," Jimmy said.

"Sorry."

"If you want to make up for it, try the door," he said.

There was no way I could back out now. And I figured I owed him one for scaring him. I reached out.  *Please be locked,* I thought over and over. I put my fingers on the knob. It was rough and rusty. I turned it. It didn't budge. "Locked," I said.

"I guess we're not going inside," Jimmy said.

"Guess not. But you can't say we didn't try." I could feel my muscles relax. I hadn't even realized how tense I was. And then, like an idiot, I turned the knob the other way.

That worked.

I glanced over at Jimmy, hoping he'd already walked far enough away that he hadn't heard the raspy sound of the latch sliding free. I could tell from his face that he'd noticed. There was no way I could pretend it hadn't happened.

I pushed the door open, hoping it wouldn't creak.

It was silent. I think that was even worse.

"Now what?" Jimmy asked.

"We go in. We walk around. And then we go home with proof," I said, holding up my phone.

"We'll be the coolest kids in school," Jimmy said.

 That thought gave me enough courage to walk inside. I tapped the flashlight icon on my phone and scanned the room. Except for a lot of dust, it could be any house.

"They say two brothers lived here," Jimmy

said. "They were always fighting with each other. One day, things got violent."

"I know. I heard the same stories you did," I said. There were all sorts of versions. None of them ended happily for the brothers.

I'd reached the stairs. I knew I'd have to go up to the second floor. That's where they said the brothers had died. But I didn't have to go up first.

I pointed up the stairs. "I opened the door. It's your turn."

"But . . ." Jimmy didn't seem to be able to come up with a good argument against this. He lifted one foot and put it on the first step like he was afraid it would collapse beneath him. He paused, then took another step.

Almost finished, I told myself as I followed him up. We would walk down the hall, peek into the rooms, and then get out as fast as we could. And I'd probably have nightmares for a month or two. But it would be over.

We had just reached the top step when the screams pierced the air.

I screamed back as I spun and saw someone running down the hall from the left. It was a kid swinging a baseball bat.

Jimmy grabbed my arm and pointed to the other end of the hall. Another kid was rushing at us wearing a hockey mask and waving a hockey stick.

Without thinking, I threw my phone at the kid on my left, as hard as I could. My jaw dropped as the phone sailed right through him and smacked against the wall.

"Ghosts!" Jimmy screamed.

We turned to run.

Our feet got tangled as we both tried to step onto the same spot.

We tumbled down the stairs and crashed to the floor. I tried to stand, but the wind was knocked out of me. I pulled myself away from the stairs with my hands, then looked back.

The ghosts were coming down the stairs.

"Let's get out of here," Jimmy said. "I'll bet they can't come outside."

I got to my feet and headed for the door, which we'd left open. I couldn't wait to get out-side and leave the ghosts behind. Everyone knows they can't leave the place they are haunting. "Phew . . ." I said as I stepped onto the porch. "That was close."

"I thought we were dead," Jimmy said.

I jumped as the flag flapped again, real hard. I spun toward it and stared. This time, there was no breeze, but the flag flapped hard, like it was trying to break free of the pole.

"Don't tell me everything is haunted, now," I said. I could picture things coming to life and startling me all the way home.

Jimmy didn't answer. He was staring across

the lawn. "Sammy . . ." he said, pointing at a skinny birch tree near the street.

I looked. The tree was bent against a strong wind. I looked all around. A piece of litter tumbled down the street, skittering like it was fleeing from a monster. The grass rippled. The flag flapped even harder.

There was a strong wind.

But I couldn't feel it. I held my hand out. "It feels calm," I said.

"Dead calm," Jimmy said.

"We can't feel the wind," I said.

Jimmy poked himself in the shoulder. "We can't feel anything," he said.

We tried to leave the porch, but we couldn't.

I looked back inside, and saw myself at the bottom of the steps. Jimmy was on the floor next to me.

"Why'd you run?" the kid with the bat asked. "We just wanted to play."

"Sorry about screaming. We got excited,"

the kid with the hockey stick said. "Hardly anybody ever comes to visit. And most of them run away from us."

It looked like the Parker house had gotten two more ghosts.

Outside, the flag drooped as the breeze died back down.

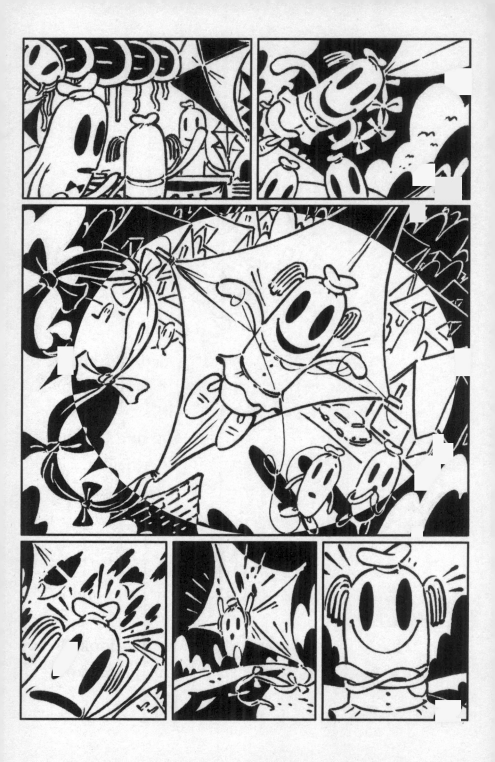

GO FLY A KITE

The summer sea breeze ruffled the kites that sat outside the shop. It sounded to Kendra like they were clapping for her. "That's the one I want," she said, pointing to a bright green model that was nearly half her height.

"It's so plain and simple," her mom said.

"It's perfect," Kendra said.

Her dad touched the chin of a fiery red dragon. "This one is amazing."

"It is," Kendra said. "But it's not the one I want."

Her mom walked over to a kite that looked like a giant goldfish splashed with a pattern of orange, yellow, white, and black. "This koi is beautiful."

"It is," Kendra said. "But I know what I want."

So her parents bought her the simple, classic kite she wanted. It was made of thin paper attached to a diamond-shaped frame of wooden sticks. The label claimed, in big bold red letters, that it was a super kite, with more lift than any kite in the world.

They headed for the beach.

"That's a strong wind," her dad said as they walked close to the edge of the water.

"Perfect," Kendra said.

Her dad held the kite while Kendra unspooled about twenty yards of line. "Ready?" he asked. He held the kite up and waited. Kendra nodded and started running.

Before she'd even run three steps, the kite took flight, shooting nearly straight up. Kendra played out more line. The kite soared higher.

"Definitely super," Kendra said.

She kept feeding out the line, and working the kite higher. There was hardly any work to it. The kite really was super, and seemed to want to climb to the clouds.

Soon, the line was all spooled out. The kite, now barely more than a green dot in the sky, tugged harder.

Kendra held on. "No! You aren't getting away!"

The kite tugged even harder.

Kendra stood on the tips of her toes, and tried to keep her arms down.

The kite was too strong. It pulled her arms up. And then, it pulled her off her feet.

"Yikes!" Kendra gasped.

 By the time she realized she should have let go, it was too late. She'd been lifted high in the air above the beach.

"Hold on!" her parents shouted.

That seemed like a good idea.

Kendra held on.

But she kept rising.

This will not end well, she thought. She laughed, because that sounded like something her dad might say. She was scared, but she realized she was also excited. It was amazing to look down at the shore and the ocean, and at the looping roller coasters on the pier.

Kendra had never been in an airplane, but she didn't think it could be anywhere near as amazing as this ride.

She tossed that thought aside as another one hit her. *I have to save myself.* She couldn't wait for someone else to get her out of this situation. She had to be her own hero. And she had to act soon. The kite was still rising, and the air was getting chilly.

There was only one thing to do. Slowly, trying not to let her

muscles get overtired, she reeled in the line, hauling herself up. Inch by inch, she moved closer to the kite. Finally, she reached it.

Kendra looked down. Then, she looked back up, because *down* was really far away. Everything seemed smaller than a model train layout.

The whole time she'd climbed the string, she'd thought about what she had to do. Now, it was time to do it. She didn't like the idea, both because it would ruin her amazing super kite, and because if it didn't work she'd be in big trouble.

"Here goes," Kendra said.

She took her pinkie and poked a tiny hole in the kite.

It jerked hard, as if wounded. Then it settled back into its rise. But the rise felt just a tiny bit less steep.

Kendra poked another small hole in the paper, at a different spot.

The rise was barely noticeable now.

Carefully, Kendra added more holes, until the kite stopped climbing and started to drop. She added one final hole, to make sure she was going down, then held on and waited.

It was almost dark when she finally touched down, seven miles away from where she'd started. A police car, an ambulance, and a fire truck were there. Everyone had been following her trip. Later, she learned they'd talked about rescuing her with a helicopter, but someone had pointed out that the wind from the blade might have caused a huge problem.

After her parents had given her as many hugs as they needed, her mom took the kite away. "We're getting rid of this one," she said.

"Don't worry," her dad said. "We'll get you another one if you still like kite flying."

"I definitely like kite flying," Kendra said. Especially when she was flown by the kite. She wondered what sort of adventure she could have, tomorrow, with that amazing dragon. Who knew where it might take her?

LOSING THE PICTURE

The worst things can happen suddenly. One moment, Neal was lying on the floor enjoying his favorite cartoon—*Whizzbang Troopers in Hyper Space*. Then, with no warning, the picture vanished. There was nothing on the screen but blackness and a dim reflection of the living room.

"Hey!" Neal said after he realized that this wasn't some great new special effect.

"What's wrong?" his sister Mary asked.

"Teebee gone," two-year-old Trina said. "No teebee."

"I'll take care of this." Neal knew that, as

the oldest, it was his job to fix the problem. He got up and searched for the remote control. The search took several minutes. Somehow, the remote was always sneaking under a couch cushion or hiding behind the bookcase. This time, the remote had burrowed under a pile of magazines on the corner table. Neal tried a different channel. There was no picture. He tried turning the TV off and on. It didn't help. He tried turning the TV off, counting to ten, then turning the TV on. That didn't help either.

"Want teebee!" Trina shouted. She started to cry.

"Do something, Neal," Mary said.

Neal thought about getting his mom. She was studying for her class and had asked them not to disturb her unless there was an emergency. Was this an emergency? It certainly seemed that way to Neal, but he still wanted to see if he could solve the problem himself. He grabbed the first thing he could find. "Trina, here, look at this." He opened the magazine

and flipped past the cover. "Look at all the pretty pictures."

"Make pictures move," Trina said.

"Sure," Neal told her. "I can make them move." He waved the magazine around and made *whoosh*ing sounds. For a moment, Trina just stared at him. Then she smiled. Then she grinned. Then she laughed.

"More," Trina said.

Neal moved the magazine around some more. "Make pictures talk," Trina said.

"I can do that." Mary took the magazine. She held it up for Trina and started telling her a story about the pictures. She just seemed to be making the tale up as she went along. Trina kept smiling and giggling. Each time Mary turned a page, she changed the story to match the picture. No matter what was there—a person, a car, a toothbrush—Mary managed to make it interesting.

Neal sat down. He enjoyed listening to Mary's story. It was full of surprises. When Mary was finished, even before Trina could shout for more, Neal took the magazine and started telling a story of his own. "This is fun," he said between stories. He liked the way he could start with nothing but a picture and dream up a whole world of pretend adventures. He also enjoyed knowing that he could make anything he wanted happen, and the story could come out just the way he wished.

"My turn," Mary said when Neal was finished. She took the magazine, flipped the pages to a picture of a stream, and started telling a story about a mermaid who lived in a creek that flowed through magic woods.

A truck pulled up outside. The screech of its brakes startled Neal. He hadn't realized how quiet it was in the house.

"I'll be right back," he said. His mom had

asked him to keep an eye out for
a package she was expecting. He
went to the porch to get it. As he
turned toward the door, he noticed
something flapping in the wind. The
wire connecting the TV to the antenna had pulled loose. That's all it
was. The antenna had become disconnected.
His mom could hook that back up in a second. Neal realized it was almost time for the
*Adventures of Captain Superblast and his Zany
Sidekicks*.

He returned to the living room, eager to
show his sisters that he had found the problem. As he walked in, Neal heard part of the
story Mary was telling about an elf who lived
inside a giant detergent box. "Guess what,"
he said proudly. He felt great that he'd
figured out the trouble all by himself.

"What?" Mary glanced up from the
magazine.

Neal looked at the blank TV
screen. He listened to the sounds in
the room. There weren't any. It was

kind of nice. "Nothing," he said. There would be plenty of time later for television. Besides, he wanted to learn what happened to the elf. He sat down on the rug and listened to his sister tell a story.

ABOUT THE AUTHOR

DAVID LUBAR credits his passion for short stories to his limited attention span and bad typing skills, though he has been known to sit still and peck at the keyboard long enough to write a novel or chapter book now and then, including *Hidden Talents* (an ALA Best Book for Young Adults) and *My Rotten Life,* which is currently under development for a cartoon series. He lives in Nazareth, Pennsylvania, with his amazing wife, and not too far from his amazing daughter. In his spare time, he takes naps on the couch.

ABOUT THE
ILLUSTRATOR

BILL MAYER is absolutely amazing. Bill's crazy creatures, characters, and comic creations have been sought after for magazine covers, countless articles, and even stamps for the U.S. Postal Service. He has won almost every illustration award known to man and even some known to fish. Bill and his wife live in Decatur, Georgia. They have a son and three grandsons.